For Danny, Kate,
and Jane
— D.M.

To Haley, Chloe,
and Ava Collier
and all children who take
the time to observe
their world
— B.C.

The illustrations for
this book were done in watercolor
and collage on 400-pound Arches watercolor
paper. The text was set in Neutra Text PS, and the
display type is Roller World BTN. • This book was edited by
Allison Moore and designed by Roberta Pressel with art direction
by Saho Fujii. The production was supervised by Erika Schwartz
and the production editor was Annie McDonnell.

Text copyright © 2016 by Diana Murray • Illustrations copyright © 2016 by Bryan Collier •
Cover art © 2016 by Bryan Collier • Cover design by Saho Fujii and Roberta Pressel • Cover
copyright © 2016 Hachette Book Group, Inc. • All rights reserved. In accordance with the U.S.
Copyright Act of 1976, the scanning, uploading, and electronic sharing of any part of this book
without the permission of the publisher is unlawful piracy and theft of the author's intellectual
property. If you would like to use material from the book (other than for review purposes), prior
written permission must be obtained by contacting the publisher at permissions@hbgusa.com.
Thank you for your support of the author's rights. • Little, Brown and Company • Hachette Book
Group • 1290 Avenue of the Americas, New York, NY 10104 • Visit us at lb-kids.com •
Little, Brown and Company is a division of Hachette Book Group, Inc. • The Little,
Brown name and logo are trademarks of Hachette Book Group, Inc. • The publisher is not
responsible for websites (or their content) that are not owned by the publisher. •
First Edition: June 2016 • Library of Congress Cataloging-in-Publication Data •
Murray, Diana. • City shapes / by Diana Murray ; illustrated by Bryan Collier. — First
edition. • pages cm • Summary: "A young girl walks through the bustling city,
while a pigeon flies above, both spotting hidden shapes at every turn"—
Provided by publisher. • ISBN 978-0-316-37092-9 (hardcover) • [1. Stories
in rhyme. 2. Shape—Fiction. 3. City and town life—Fiction.
4. Pigeons—Fiction.] I. Collier, Bryan, illustrator. II. Title.
PZ8.3.M9362Cit 2016 • [E]—dc23 • 2015000410 •
10 9 8 7 6 5 4 3 2 1 • APS •
PRINTED IN CHINA

CITY SHAPES

By **Diana Murray**

Illustrated by **Bryan Collier**

LITTLE, BROWN AND COMPANY

New York   Boston

A pigeon takes flight through the bright cityscape,
exploring the scenery . . . **SHAPE** after **SHAPE**.

The city is bursting with **SHAPES** of each kind.
And if you look closely, who knows what you'll find!

A truck rumbling by
to deliver the mail,
a silvery cart with
hot pretzels for sale,

and stacks of brown
packages hauled up
the stairs . . .

Some **SHAPES** in the city are . . .

on-the-go SQUARES.

A skyscraper covered in shimmering glass,
a long metal bench near a green patch of grass,
and a table with glittery scarves and gold bangles . . .

Some **SHAPES**
in the city are . . .
dazzling
RECTANGLES.

The seaport with all of its flowing white sails,
and there, in the market, the pointy fish tails,
and colorful flags on a banner that dangles . . .

Some **SHAPES** in the city are . . .
gleaming **TRIANGLES**.

The sunglasses worn by a cop on his beat,
the wheels of the taxis that zip down the street,
and a manhole that leads to the pipes underground . . .

Some **SHAPES**
in the city are . . .
CIRCLES,
so round.

At sunset the city is softly aglow
as chitchatting crowds hustle-bustle below,
when off in the distance a melody hums.
It's hard not to follow the sound of the drums.

The stage in the park where the instruments sing—
some **SHAPES** in the city are . . .
OVALS that swing.

And nearby, the kites seem to dance in the sky.

Some **SHAPES** in the city are . . .
DIAMONDS that fly.

The sun fades away into
hazy blue dark,
and soon there's a twinkle,
a glimmer, a spark.

Scattered up high, above
buildings and cars—

Some SHAPES in the city are
faraway STARS.

The pigeon flies back through the night cityscape
as city lights sparkle, SHAPE after SHAPE.
But her heart starts to ache for the SHAPE
she loves best.
The SHAPE that is *home*—

her warm **CIRCLE** nest . . .

where the whirring and beeping of cars rushing by
helps her fall fast asleep, like a sweet lullaby.

AUTHOR'S NOTE

I was born in Ukraine and immigrated to New York City at the age of two. I lived in a tall building with a balcony that gave me a bird's-eye view of the neighborhood. Sometimes I even got to wave to my friend on a balcony across the street. For many years after college, I lived in busy midtown Manhattan, where parades regularly marched under my window and the familiar ebb and flow of city traffic lulled me to sleep each night.

On weekends, I often took a "hike" around the city (hiking boots and all!), walking for miles, all the way down to Chinatown and back again. I loved the way the neighborhoods changed, the diversity of the architecture, the people, and the interesting discoveries around every corner. That was my inspiration for writing this book. I recently moved to a nearby suburb with my two wonderful daughters and my husband, who is a New York City fire chief. It's fun to have my very own backyard, but whenever I go back to the city, it still feels like home.

Diana Murray

ARTIST'S NOTE

City Shapes is a wondrous journey of discovery through the eyes of our young tour guide as she shows off as much of her world as she can in the span of a full day. This little girl (who happens to be my four-year-old daughter) leads us throughout her neighborhood, urging us to notice things we hadn't spotted before: some shapes that we will recognize right away and some that require a closer look. Meanwhile, a bird flies above, reminding us that there's always another perspective to consider.

The art for this book was done in watercolor and collage on 400-pound Arches watercolor paper. I think collage works so well with this story because it illuminates all the smaller elements and shapes to form a whole picture. When I read this text for the first time, I was immediately inspired. In this kaleidoscope of colors and shapes, I hope you can almost hear and taste the sounds and smells of this vibrant and colorful city day. And as night falls and the stars come out, you'll see how city and nature combine in a gentle mix of new tones and shapes to discover.

B. Potter